Zebra's Tent

Written and illustrated by
Laura Hambleton

Collins

3

Sheep got snacks from his bright red backpack.

"Yum, sweets!" said Croc.

Zebra got cups for the drink and Duck got spoons for the yogurt.

"Look at my pink and green dressing up box" said Zebra.

Croc took the bright green hat.
"I'm looking good!" he boasted.

Sheep sang a sweet song and Duck had a bang on the drum.

Zebra said, "We must sleep soon.
It is dark."

"I will sweep up the mess," said Sheep,
getting a broom.

Duck collected the green sheets
and Croc got the books.

"Is it a thunderstorm?" said Croc in fright.
"Or a spook?" said Sheep, feeling afraid.

"It is not a spook! It is my mum!"
said Zebra.

Mum had mugs and brown toast.

Yum!

Zebra's tent

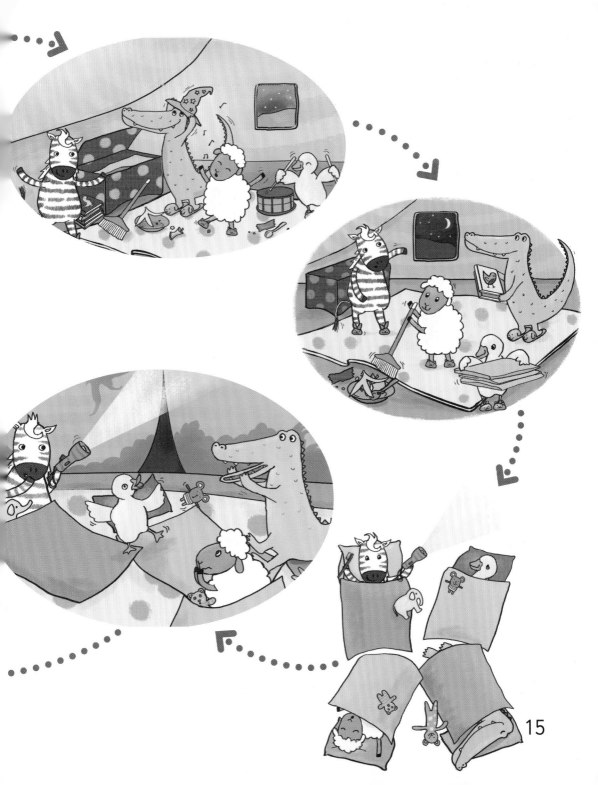

After reading

Letters and Sounds: Phase 4

Word count: 169

Focus on adjacent consonants with long vowel phonemes, e.g. /g/ /r/ /ee/ /n/

Common exception words: the, I, my, he, we, be, said, to

Curriculum links: PSHE

National Curriculum learning objectives: Reading/word reading: apply phonic knowledge and skills as the route to decode words; read accurately by blending sounds in unfamiliar words containing GPCs that have been taught; read other words of more than one syllable that contain taught GPCs; Reading/comprehension: understand both the books they can already read accurately and fluently and those they listen to by making inferences on the basis of what is being said and done

Developing fluency

- Your child may enjoy hearing you read the book.
- Read the book to your child out loud with expression, using different voices for the animals.
- On pages 10 and 11, take turns to read the main text and noises. For page 11, encourage your child to use expression to show how the animals are feeling.

Phonic practice

- Look through the book together to find words that begin with adjacent consonants that have different phonemes (letter sounds). (e.g. *stars, bright*)
- Repeat for words that end with adjacent consonants that have the same phonemes (letter sounds). (e.g. *spoons*)
- Take turns with your child to point to and read words from the book that contain two syllables. (e.g. *back/pack, yo/gurt*)

Extending vocabulary

- Look at pages 6 and 7. Ask your child some questions, focusing on specific words, such as:
  - What is a **dressing up box**? (*a box with clothes to play in*)
  - Which word tells us that Croc is showing off? (*boasted*)
  - Can you think of a word that means the same as **sweet** to describe the sheep's song? (e.g. *pretty, nice*)